Genovesa

Ecuador

GALÁPAGOS
ISLANDS

SOUTH
AMERICA

Pacific Ocean

Ecuador

GALÁPAGOS
ISLANDS

SOUTH
AMERICA

Pacific Ocean

GALÁPAGOS
GEORGE

San Cristóbal

Española

To the memory of Jean Craighead George, who has given the gift of nature to generations of children. Her books remain timeless and continue to inspire. It has been my honor to be her friend and illustrator for more than twenty years. Thank you, Jean.

—W.M.

Jean Craighead George

Galápagos George

Paintings by Wendell Minor

HARPER
An Imprint of HarperCollinsPublishers

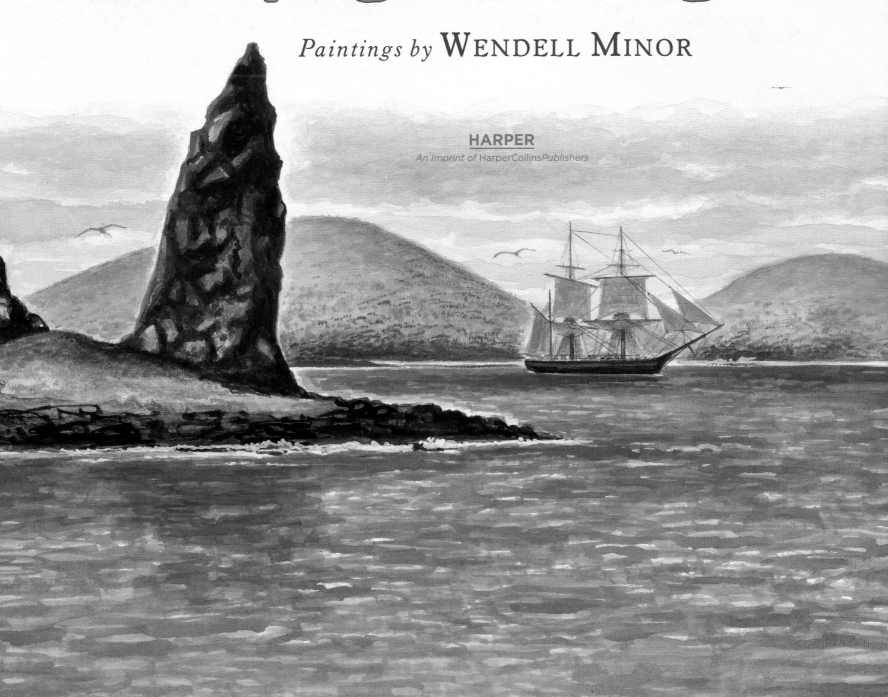

THIS IS A STORY that took so long to happen that only the stars were present at the beginning and at the end.

Around one million years ago, a giant tortoise lived in South America. Giantess George was a vegetarian who ate prickly things like cacti and ground-growing greens that grew in her ancient desert.

Giantess George saw earthquakes crack open the land. She saw mountains begin to rise and volcanoes erupt. She watched furry animals, large and small, run over the footprints of the long-vanished dinosaurs.

Then a storm struck South America. It poured
down seas of rain. It rolled the ocean up onto the
land. The ocean roared back to the sea, sweeping
away trees, cacti, and many kinds of living things.
Among them was Giantess George.

She was tumbled into the purple-black ocean.
She swirled down into whirlpools. She spun
underwater with the land creatures—iguanas,
lizards, and the furry mammals, large and small.

And then she surfaced. And she did something new. She floated. Soon she found a raft of floating trees and climbed aboard. Several sisters, brothers, and offspring also found rafts and climbed aboard.

Giantess George and the other tortoises drifted west on the sea current.

There was no tortoise food or fresh water on the tree raft, but the giantess did not die.

She did something ordinary for a tortoise. She changed her body fat into water and food. She was a desert dweller and could live for a year without eating or drinking.

She drifted for days.

Then something new happened again. The raft stopped. Her feet touched land. She came ashore on a small island six hundred miles from home, later named San Cristóbal. Several relatives landed with her. All were the same kind of tortoise. All were Giantess Georges. They ate the greens growing on the islands.

The island was nestled close to the hot equator. The weather was either terribly hot, terribly wet, or terribly dry.

Over hundreds of years, some of the tortoises were washed to sea during storms, and the currents carried them to other islands.

On a hot July dawn a million years ago, Giantess George laid twelve tennis-ball-sized eggs a bit inland and covered them over with soil.

She lived on that island very much as she had in South America. She arose at eight in the morning, ate all day, and went to sleep at four in the afternoon.

One year she ran out of ground plants. Giantess George was lucky. Her neck was a little longer than the necks of the other tortoises. She did something new. She reached up and ate tree leaves.

When she was almost two hundred years old, Giantess George died. But she left behind long-necked offspring who had longer-necked offspring, who had even longer-necked offspring.

After many thousands of years all the tortoises on her island had long, graceful necks and shells that fanned back like handsome collars. They could reach up and eat without hitting their shells with their necks. They no longer looked just like Giantess George. They were something new.

On other islands the tortoises had also changed. Some had sculptured shells. Others were domed, and still others were squat. Long necks had long necks on their island. Domed backs had domed backs on their island. They had become fourteen different kinds of tortoises all isolated from one another.

More time passed.

It was the Age of Exploration. In 1535, the bishop of Panama accidentally discovered the islands of the giant tortoises. They became known as the Galápagos Islands, the "Islands of the Tortoises."

Later, people began to arrive by the shiploads. Sailors and pirates captured and ate the tortoises, and whalers carried away many thousands. Rats ran off the ships and dug up tortoise eggs. Sea captains set goats loose to grow up and become a future food supply. The goats ate the plants the tortoises needed. Farmers settled the islands, and their pigs gobbled hatchling tortoises.

Too quickly, the 200,000 giant tortoises were reduced to mere thousands.

Years passed. One day one of the few remaining descendants of Giantess George crawled out of his eggshell and climbed up through the dirt to the sunlight. Charles Darwin, the great naturalist, walked past him. Darwin was deep in thought. Why were the giant tortoises so different on each island and yet so much alike? Darwin realized that these modern species must have had an ancient common ancestor.

For the tortoises, it was Giantess George and her kin.

Only one hundred years later, people, rats, pigs, and goats had wiped out two kinds of these magnificent tortoises, while volcanic eruptions wiped out a third. Only one of the descendants of Giantess George remained, on Pinta Island.

Then one day in the early 1970s, a scientist found a long-necked tortoise on Pinta Island. Six men lifted him into a boat and brought him to the Charles Darwin Research Station on Santa Cruz Island. Here the Galápagos tortoises are protected.

He was the last descendant of Giantess George. The scientists named him Lonesome George.

While he lived at the refuge, he ate leaves and cactus fruit. Scientists hunted the zoos of the world looking for a mate for him.

Another was never found.

At four o'clock on June 23, 2012, Lonesome George
pulled his head into his shell and put up his knees.
Peering out at the setting sun were two bright eyes.

They seemed to say: "New and unimaginable things
can happen."

Lonesome George passed away on June 24, 2012.
He was the last of his kind. But because of him and
the tortoises of the Galápagos Islands, we know that
as long as there is life, there will always be "new and
unimaginable things that can happen." And they do.
All the time.

Find Out More about Lonesome George

KEY TERMS

- **Lonesome George** was the last of the Pinta Island saddleback tortoises.

- **Adaptation** is the process by which plants or animals change to become better suited to their habitat.

- **Charles Darwin** was an English naturalist who proposed the theory that organisms have common ancestors and that they evolve
- or change over time as successful traits are passed on from one generation to the next.

- **Domed tortoises** live on islands in the Galápagos that are higher, wetter, and greener. They are able to find enough food on ground level. They did not evolve shells shaped like the saddleback tortoises'.

- **Evolution** is the process of passing on traits from one generation to the next.

- **HMS *Beagle*** is the name of the ship that Charles Darwin traveled on for five years from 1831 to 1836. His visit to the Galápagos helped to inspire his lifelong work and his book *On the Origin of Species*.

- **Pinta Island** is one of the northernmost of the Galápagos Islands and was home to Lonesome George.

- **Saddleback tortoises**, including Lonesome George, developed long necks and flared shells that allowed them to graze on cacti that were higher up than the domed-shell tortoises could reach.

TIMELINE

- **3 million years ago:** The islands that make up the Galápagos Islands as they are now were formed. There were older islands, but they are now seamounts beneath the ocean surface.

- **1535:** The bishop of Panama, Tomás de Berlanga, is credited with discovering the Galápagos. But history shows that earlier, a pre-Columbian Inca named Tupac Yupanqui also found a group of islands, which could have been the Galápagos.

- **Eighteenth and nineteenth centuries:** Buccaneers, pirates, and whalers stopping by the islands hunted tortoises for fresh meat. It is estimated that they killed nearly 200,000 of the slow-moving tortoises. They also introduced rats, cats, dogs, pigs, and goats, which have destroyed much of the native habitat.

- **1835:** Charles Darwin visited the Galápagos Islands. David Stanbury, a scholar, notes that while there, Darwin most likely witnessed Halley's Comet, which passed closest to Earth on October 13, 1835. Darwin wrote the single word "comet" in his notebook at this time. He also wrote that he saw an "immense Turpin (tortoise)" and that it "took little notice of me."

- **1906:** Samples from three of Lonesome George's ancestors were taken by scientists from the California Academy of Sciences. Recently these samples helped scientists look for mates that were closely related to the Pinta Island tortoises.

- **1912:** Lonesome George hatched close to this date, maybe a few years earlier.

- **1959:** The government of Ecuador created the Galápagos National Park to protect tortoises and their habitat.

- **1972:** Lonesome George, the last of his species, was brought to live at the Charles Darwin Research Station in hopes of finding him a mate.

- **2012:** Lonesome George died.

RESOURCES

Books:

- *Galápagos: Islands Born of Fire*, by Tui de Roy. Princeton, NJ: Princeton University Press, 2010. Written by one of the world's top wildlife photographers, this tenth-anniversary edition combines spectacular photographs with personal memories and stories about the Galápagos Islands, where she once lived.

- *Island: A Story of the Galápagos*, by Jason Chin. New York: Roaring Brook Press, a Neal Porter Book, 2012. This "biography" of an island follows it from geological birth to "adulthood" and beyond. It will generate many questions. Wonderful, accurate, beautifully illustrated.

Websites:

- **www.a-z-animals.com/animals**: Good pictures and clear, short paragraphs of information.

- **www.amnh.org**: The American Museum of Natural History has various types of information. Start by searching for "Galápagos tortoise."

- **darwin-online.org.uk**: This site contains an excellent biography as well as all of Darwin's writings and 2,000 of his drawings.

- **www.findingdulcinea.com**: Search "Galápagos" for interesting articles about the history of the Galápagos Islands, Darwin, and the issues facing the Galápagos.

- **www.galapagos.org**: The Galápagos Conservancy site has information about Lonesome George, the Galápagos Islands, and how to support the preservation of the islands.

- **www.geo.cornell.edu**: Search "Galápagos." This Cornell University website contains information about the Galápagos Islands' geography, history, geology, and ecology.

- **www.pbs.org/safarchive/galapagos.html**: Extensive information about the Galápagos, tortoises, and Darwin. You can even take a virtual expedition of the Galápagos with Scientific American Frontiers by clicking on "Cyber Field Trip."

- **www.sandiegozoo.org**: The San Diego Zoo has clear information and excellent photos about an extensive list of species. Galápagos tortoises are included. Search "Galapagos tortoise."

Do Your Own Research:

Jean George would go to see the places and animals she wrote about. While not everyone can get to the Galápagos Islands, most of us can get to a zoo or an aquarium.

Go see a tortoise! Watch it move, blink, and chew. Look at its shell: Is it flared like Lonesome George's? Is it domed? What is the tortoise eating? How is it eating? If there is a volunteer or zoo staff person nearby, ask him or her to tell you about the tortoise. Stay as long as you can, then go home, think about all you have read and learned, and write or tell your own story about the tortoise you saw.

This book meets the Common Core State Standards for English Language Arts/Science and Technical Subjects.

✦ IN REMEMBRANCE ✦

Jean Craighead George and Lonesome George passed away within weeks of each other in 2012. They were both one of a kind.

Jean wrote to awaken an interest in and love for wild things and wild places. To place the reader in the environments she described. To make us feel the magnificence and importance of all organisms and habitats, no matter how small, or barren, or few in number.

Lonesome George was the last of the Pinta Island tortoises in the Galápagos Islands. He inspired many to help preserve the Galápagos and all its tortoises and to hope for a future in which humans and nature will live in abundant balance with each other.

They will both be missed, but their messages will be carried on in new and unimaginable ways, every day, by all of us.

—*Twig George*

The artist wishes to thank several friends who provided many wonderful reference photos from their trips to the Galápagos. My thanks go to Roger Straus, Doris Straus, Andy Shapiro, Carolyn Setlow, and Jean Craighead George.

—Wendell Minor

Special thanks to Dr. Linda Cayot, Galápagos Conservancy Science Advisor, for her valuable assistance.

Library of Congress Cataloging-in-Publication Data. George, Jean Craighead, date. Galapagos George / Jean Craighead George ; paintings by Wendell Minor. — 1st ed.   p.   cm. ISBN 978-0-06-028793-1 (trade bdg.) ISBN 978-0-06-028794-8 (lib. bdg.) 1. Galapagos tortoise—Juvenile literature.   2. Galapagos tortoise—Evolution—Juvenile literature.   3. Galapagos tortoise—Migration—Juvenile literature.   I. Minor, Wendell, ill. II. Title. QL666. C584G46 2014   2011030446   597.92'46—dc23   CIP   AC

The artist used Windsor and Newton Watercolors on archival 3-ply Strathmore Bristol paper to create the illustrations for this book.

Typography by Dana Fritts. 13 14 15 16 17 SCP 10 9 8 7 6 5 4 3 2 1 ❖ First Edition